Sophie

❧ BOOK 1 ☙

Orphan Train Series

Wendy May Andrews

☙❧

Sparrow Ink
www.sparrowink.com

ISBN – 978-1-989634-58-5

www.wendymayandrews.com

Stay in touch with Wendy May Andrews
and forthcoming publishing news.

Sign up for her biweekly newsletter

Introduction

His pursuit of her threatens everything – except her heart.

Sophie Brooks has lived at the orphanage since she was ten years old. Now nineteen, she's not only a resident, she works there as well. It's the only true home she can remember and she'll do whatever it takes to keep it safe.

When her budding relationship with the son of one of the orphanage's benefactors threatens the charity's funding, Sophie must choose between her loyalties and her heart.

To all those yearning for a better life – May you find the happy ever after you're searching for.

To Mum and Dad for being excited about my orphans and heroines and helping me round out my stories.

To Marlene and Suzanne for being such great critiquers.

And last, but certainly not least, to Mr. Andrews for being the very best always.

Chapter 1

New York City, spring 1854

“Sophie! Wait up!”

As she heard the familiar voice, her heart rate picked up, but so did her feet. Without turning to acknowledge his call, Sophie did her best to hurry away. Of course, hampered by her layers of skirts to ward off the chill and her much shorter legs, her effort was wasted. He quickly caught up to her.

“Good morning, Sophie. How are you this morning? I called out for you, but you must not have heard me.”

“Good morning, Mr. Rexford,” she acknowledged politely, not slowing her pace.

He paused in his stride but then hurried to catch up to her. “Sophie, are you trying to get away from me? What's going on with you this morning?"

She wanted to tell him that yes, she *was* trying to get away from him, but that would only raise more questions from him. She needed to be wily, she reminded herself. He mustn't find out the truth.

"Of course not, everything is just fine," she finally answered him, trying to infuse her voice with as much sincerity as possible, even though she couldn't quite meet his eye. "I'm just in a bit of a hurry. It's my turn to collect the donations from the bakery for the children today, and I'm afraid I'm going to be late."

"Well, then I'll come with you and help you carry it. That way it will be easier for you, and then we can talk as we walk."

His deep voice, obviously trying to sound reasonable, made her breath catch in her throat, and Sophie had to will the tears to remain behind her eyelids where they belonged. He could not sense her emotions or it would spoil everything. She cast him a tight smile. "That's kind of you to offer, Mr. Rexford, but I really cannot tarry. I will wish you a good day." She offered him a small nod before picking up her skirt and willing her legs to move even faster without actually breaking into a run.

Thankfully, her primness had gotten through to him sufficiently that he stopped in his tracks. She could feel his gaze on her back but managed to control herself so that she didn't turn back to glance at him or wave or in any other way indicate the turmoil churning in her chest.

Sophronia Brooks, Sophie to her friends, finally stopped to catch her breath, leaning wearily against the corner of a building and pulling her skirts in around her to prevent them from being brushed by the bustle that continued on around her. Renton, that is, Mr. Rexford, would have been useful to have with her. She would have felt safer, for one important thing. And with his much larger build, he would have been of great assistance to her in carrying what was sure to be a large gift from the bakery. But she needed to dismiss the thought, she reminded herself. Mr. Renton Robert Rexford the Third was not for her. And no matter how much she enjoyed his company or how much he seemed to enjoy hers, he was never going to be for her, and she needed to get that realization through her thick skull.

With that determination, she stepped away from the wall, straightened her shoulders, raised her chin, loosened her grip on her skirts, and strode purposefully toward her destination. Besides, she reminded herself, she didn't need a man's company in order to accomplish her task.

She was out at the safest time of the day and was marching along the safest route possible. Nothing about her would proclaim her as a likely target for anyone. There was nothing for her to fear, and even though his company would have been nice, she was good enough company for herself. She didn't need Mr. Rexford, or anyone. She, Sophie Brooks, was all she needed. *And don't you forget it*, she reprimanded herself.

Before long, she arrived at her destination. She quickly glanced at her reflection in the glass of the neighboring shop. Despite the accumulated grime on the window, Sophie was able to see that her cheeks were rosy from her brisk walk and the crisp air but that her speed hadn't disrupted much of the tight knot she had twisted her unruly chestnut curls into. She looked sufficiently neat and tidy, despite the pink that tinged the tip of her nose, not to cause offense to the shopkeeper who was being so generous to the orphanage.

Stale doughnuts wouldn't be most people's idea of a treat, but the children at the orphanage would be delighted when they found them served that evening. Sophie wished she could hold her breath while she was at the bakery; smelling all that sweet deliciousness only made her wish for what could not be. But such was life. She braced her shoulders once more. She hesitated for a moment, though. Should she go to the front door or the back? She had forgotten to ask when Mrs. Parker had sent her on this errand. She glanced at her reflection once more. There was nothing terribly off putting about her appearance, so even if she ought to be at the back, she doubted it would offend the shopkeeper if she came in the front. At least she certainly hoped not. It was tricky business receiving charity.

With a polite smile pinned to her face, Sophie hoped for the best and opened the door, inhaling deeply of the sweet, doughy aroma permeating the bright shop. It just couldn't be helped. She stood still for a second, taking another deep, appreciative sniff but then stepped to the counter. She was fortunate, there was an obvious lull in the shop's business, and there was only one customer being cared for at the moment.

"Can I help you, miss?" The shopkeeper turned to her as his customer stepped away.

"Good morning, I'm Sophie from the Foundling Hospital." She kept her smile polite and her gaze unwavering even though the man's expression changed from being eager for new business to disappointment.

"Fine. Come through here. We have a sack prepared for you." He eyed her speculatively. "You going to be able to manage on your own? Should've sent a man for this."

Again, Sophie kept her smile polite and in place. She was quite used to being underestimated. And there were never enough men to help with the work that needed to be done. This was probably going to be one of the less onerous assignments she had been given, so she didn't bother replying. When she saw the sack he indicated, she worked hard to fight her dismay. She only wished it were bigger, even if it would have been harder to carry. From the looks of it, they wouldn't be able to offer each child a doughnut of their own. With a mental shrug, she decided half a doughnut would please the children almost as much.

Sophie grabbed the sack and nodded to the man. "Thank you for your generosity, sir, the children will be delighted."

The baker merely grunted in acknowledgement before frowning and demanding, "You sure you can manage? Looks to me like you'll blow away with the wind. I'm not sure I should be sending my product off with you."

Now Sophie was starting to get irritated. Part of her wanted to stamp her foot and use colorful language, but she struggled to keep her face serene. "I'm quite certain I shall be fine, sir. I appreciate your concern. Good day." Without waiting for any further doubts to be uttered by the obtuse man, she turned away and exited through the conveniently propped open back door. She could have told him the bag was only half full so it wouldn't be any trouble at all for her to manage, but she had been told a myriad of times by Mr. Brace and the directors of the Children's Aid Society that they could never look a gift horse in the mouth. She always needed to be grateful for whatever was offered to them, no matter how she might wish otherwise.

With a sigh, as soon as she was away from the shop, Sophie swung the sack up over her shoulder, making it a simple task to carry it. She understood that she looked small. It had always been the bane of her existence. Being small was forever causing people to underestimate her. Of course, that could, on occasion, work to her advantage, but it was usually a pain rather than a pleasure. But it didn't matter today. Her size wasn't much of a factor. And the size of her bundle would prevent any undue attention to be drawn toward her. She should be able to return to the orphanage without any trouble at all. As long as she didn't run into Renton again. That had been unnecessarily awkward. Sophie sighed again as she failed to suppress her memories of the first time she had met Renton.

It was the Winter Formal that Mrs. Rexford, Renton's mother, had planned in her continued efforts to raise money for the Foundling Hospital.

Mrs. Rexford was one of the Children's Aid Society's biggest donors. Since the Society was such a new organization, Mr. Brace was dependent on the woman's generosity. Mr. Brace had invited Sophie to join a few of the other staff members at the event. She had been beside herself with excitement and had spent hours with some of the older girls at the orphanage planning her clothes and hair for the evening. It had been such a joy to share it with the children. Even though they couldn't attend, they had been nearly as excited as Sophie herself.

Sophie's heart clenched as she remembered how even the most sober of the girls had giggled along with her as they helped her pin up her hair in what was surely the most elegant style her curls had ever managed. It had been like a fairy tale. If only they would all get their happily ever after. Her musings continued.

Sophie arrived in the center of the cluster of staff members who would be attending. She had to exert considerable effort to keep her jaw from dropping open as she gazed about at the most beautiful room she had ever seen. Mrs. Rexford was standing ready to greet her guests as they entered. Always polite, Sophie approached her to express her appreciation.

"Everything looks so amazing, Mrs. Rexford. Thank you for including us in your evening."

Mrs. Rexford's smile didn't quite reach her eyes, but Sophie didn't pay it much heed at the moment.

"Of course, Sophie, I'm sure you'll have an enjoyable evening."

Sophie was a little confused as to how to reply to those words. She nodded and dipped a slight curtsy before turning away, trying not to allow a frown to form on her brow. She understood she needed to represent the orphanage well.

She was just pinning what she hoped was a gracious smile back onto her face while scanning the gathering crowd, looking for the rest of her group, when her gaze collided with that of the most handsome man she had ever seen. His blue eyes were so clear and bright, they reminded her of the Atlantic on a sunny day. His dark hair was almost black and was clipped short. It looked as though it would have a tendency to curl if he had not controlled its length. His square jaw and high cheekbones should have looked fierce, but his lips quirked up in the corners as though he had a propensity for smiling or laughing. Sophie's breath caught as she tried to take it all in and once again found herself hoping her mouth wasn't hanging open.

He strode toward her, as she was frozen in place. There wasn't much space separating them, so he was beside her in a few paces.

"Good evening, miss. I haven't had the pleasure of making your acquaintance. I just saw you talking with my mother."

Sophie blinked and almost turned to look behind her before she remembered that she had just been speaking with Mrs. Rexford. Feeling a blush stain her cheeks, Sophie tried to achieve coherent speech, but nothing intelligent came to mind so she merely offered him a slight curtsy like she had done with his mother.

"Oh no, let's not be formal, I beg of you." His words surprised a laugh out of Sophie. She was even more surprised by the embarrassment that stained his cheeks as his grin turned rueful. "Are you laughing because my mother has called this event a Formal? And now I'm begging you not to be formal?"

Sophie just smiled at him. She still didn't have any words to offer. He didn't seem to mind her silence. He caught her hand and tucked it into his elbow.

"It's getting a bit crowded in here. I could escort you to your table."

Finally, Sophie's brain became unfrozen. Even though she didn't pull her hand from his elbow, she offered a half-hearted protest. "I couldn't possibly occupy your time, Mr. Rexford. Surely you have others you need to be speaking with."

"Not at all, my mother has everything under control. All I need to do is show up to these things."

"Does your mother host parties like this regularly?" Sophie couldn't even imagine it.

"Certainly. It is her greatest" —he paused almost imperceptibly before finishing— "joy."

Sophie was fascinated by his hesitation but didn't feel brave enough to question him. She allowed her gaze to circle the room once more. "Her experience has paid off. She is certainly very skilled. Everything is beautiful, and everyone seems to be happy to be here."

"Are you happy to be here?"

"Absolutely." Sophie's reply was filled with conviction. She doubted she would have the opportunity again and was determined to wring every drop of enjoyment she could from the experience. The man at her side returned her grin.

"How rude of me, I haven't introduced myself," he said, turning the subject. *"I'm Renton Rexford, of Rexford and Associates."*

Sophie nodded graciously in acknowledgement. "I'm Sophie Brooks." She hesitated for a second before adding, "Of the Foundling Hospital."

His eyes widened in surprise, but his reception of her hadn't noticeably cooled, much to Sophie's surprised relief. "Are you one of the orphans? You don't look like a child, I must say."

Sophie grinned. "Thank you, kind sir. I am an orphan, or I guess you could say I was. Mr. Brace has allowed me to stay on and work there now that I am grown."

Mr. Rexford didn't ask any more questions just then. "It is a pleasure to make your acquaintance, Miss Brooks. Are you seated with the rest of Mr. Brace's group, then?"

"I would imagine so. I stopped to speak with Mrs. Rexford, and the others went ahead without me."

"That was rude of them," he observed.

Sophie giggled softly. "Not at all. They probably didn't notice I had stopped. And surely I cannot get lost in one large open room."

He patted her hand where it sat in the crook of his elbow and then left his hand covering hers. Sophie's stomach fluttered at the contact. She was torn between relief that she was wearing gloves and a desperate wish that neither of them had their hands covered so that she could get the full sensation. It was a ridiculous thought since she would not have been considered properly attired if she had not worn gloves and thus would not have been allowed entrance.

Sophie tried to stem the flow of these vivid memories. They caused such a cacophony of pleasure and pain as she thought back to that exquisite evening.

He took her the long way around the room, even though he professed to know where Mr. Brace's group had been seated. When they reached one corner of the room, Sophie allowed her gaze to scan the room and was surprised to see Mr. Brace in the direct opposite corner, the farthest away possible.

"Oh Mr. Renton, I do apologize. I believe my group is quite far away."

He grinned at her. "Why would you apologize?"

"Well, if you are truly going to escort me all the way, that is surely going to occupy your time needlessly."

"Like I told you, I know exactly where Mr. Brace has been seated."

Sophie frowned at him. "Are you perfectly sure?"

"Yes, and we will get there in due time." He must have noticed her puzzled frown because he gave her a lopsided grin that made the flutters in her tummy start up again. "I didn't think you were

in a rush, and I wanted to enjoy the pleasure of your company a little while longer."

Sophie protested no further. She had no wish to hurry him on his way. She had never enjoyed such a moment of bliss as she listened to him discretely explain who the various people were as they passed them. He entertained her with amusing anecdotes about the people she had only heard tell of prior. She would have enjoyed walking on his arm even if they had walked for miles. But even though the room had seemed vast when she had first stepped foot into it, and even though he had gone the longest way around possible, long before she was ready for it to be over, they arrived at her table. She introduced him politely to her friends and colleagues. Mr. Brace had cast her a quizzical glance but didn't comment until Mr. Rexford was far enough away, after Sophie had taken her seat next to him.

"How does it happen that Renton Rexford the Third was escorting you to our table, Sophie, my dear?"

Shaking her head and shrugging lightly, she tried to answer. "I have no idea, Mr. Brace. It seemed to happen quite by accident."

He looked torn between worry for her and glee, which caused Sophie to wrinkle her nose at him. Mr. Brace laughed. "Be very careful, my dear girl, but maybe you can encourage them to open their purse strings a little bit further."

Grinning but shaking her head, Sophie turned her attention to the rest of the table. Everyone looked so nice. Nothing like their usual, serviceable clothing. Even their facial expressions looked different. Mrs. Parker, usually so prim and anxious, with about ten things too many to accomplish in any given moment, looked relaxed for the first time in Sophie's memory.

"Have you been to one of Mrs. Rexford's gatherings before?" Sophie asked, hoping to divert attention away from her arrival on Mr. Rexford's escort.

"Yes, once before. You are in for a treat, Sophie. The food will far surpass anything you have ever tasted. Definitely far better than anything we can ever produce from our kitchens."

"Maybe we could ask Mrs. Rexford to give us some tips."

Mrs. Parker laughed but shook her head at Sophie. "You are such a dreamer, my dear."

Sophie blinked in surprise, wondering why she would react in that way. Before she could question Mrs. Parker, though, someone began ringing a bell. Looking all the way down to the end of the room and seeing a man preparing to make some announcements, Sophie realized that their table was the furthest away from any action. They most likely wouldn't be able to hear much of what was about to be said. She didn't allow it to bother her though. If she couldn't hear, no one could expect her to pay attention, she thought with an impish feeling. All the better to be able to take the time to gaze about at the beautiful room.

As she thought about that first encounter, Sophie remembered that she *had* looked around at the stunning architecture and chandeliers as well as the well dressed people nearby. But again and again, her eyes were drawn to the handsome man standing beside his mother, looking serious, and delicious, and approachable. Sophie giggled at the thought, even though she knew she shouldn't even be thinking about the man. But despite who he was and how good looking he was, he really was an approachable person. It was one of the things she liked best about him.

With a shake of her head, she pushed the thoughts away. It mattered very little. There was nothing to be done about it. He would have to accept her disinterest. And if he didn't, it mattered even less, since she would be getting on the train in a little over a week and would then be gone for at least a month.

Maybe she ought to take Katie and Melanie up on their offer to stay with them in Bucklin, Missouri after they escort the shipment of orphans to their new lives. No one could argue that she didn't need a fresh start. But what little a life she had was here in New York City. She didn't know if she was brave enough to start over from scratch like those two were planning. She had already done that more than once in her short life. It had been forced upon her before. Sophie didn't think she would voluntarily choose to uproot and start over even if it held a certain appeal.

Living at the Foundling Hospital wasn't the most prosperous life available, that was for certain, but it was the life she had and knew, and well, loved. It was as though she had scores of younger siblings. And she felt as though she were making a difference in their little lives, helping them to adjust to their new circumstances, whether they were newly orphaned or just newly off the street.

She had been one of Mr. Brace's earliest achievements, he was often telling her. When he opened the Foundling Hospital, she was the first girl he had admitted. And she had stuck. Making herself as helpful as possible had ensured security for herself. Now that she was nineteen, she was trying to convince herself she didn't have to be quite so insecure about her future, but in some ways it felt less secure than ever. Mr. Brace would never turn out one of the children. But since she was no longer a child, she was fearful that he might no longer have a place for her. His suggestions of arranging an apprenticeship for her were probably well intended, and she ought to take him up on it, but she truly just wanted to stay safely tucked up in the attics of the Foundling Hospital. *Is that really too much to ask?*

Her restless musings had kept her company all the way back, and she was surprised to find herself already home. She looked up at the imposing building, attempting to be unbiased as she gazed at it. She wondered if others would think it ugly and stark. But she couldn't; she was completely biased. She loved this place with her whole heart. It was the most stable home she could remember ever having. Her mother's stories of their prestigious background were most likely fairy tales, since she couldn't remember anything before they found themselves destitute and alone on the meaner side of the city before her mother got sick. Her poor, sweet mother. Mama had never ceased promising that Papa would return for them, but when she died, all her stories went with her. Sophie didn't have time for fairy tales. She would rather accomplish something practical and have food in her belly wend a warm, dry place to sleep, thank you very much.

'Stop dawdling, girl,' she could almost hear Cook bellowing at her. Sophie needed to get her prize down to the kitchen so it could be dealt with before the next meal. She hurried around to the back of the building to enter there before running up to her room to wash her face and hands.

"Were you accosted on your way back?" Cook demanded as he eyed the half full sack.

Sophie smiled at his obvious attempt to make light. "No, the bakery overestimated their generosity, I think. This was all there was when I got there."

"Humph. We should have gone last night. He probably sold off some of his stale stock as fresh to some poor, unsuspecting customer."

Sophie wanted to shrug but merely nodded in agreement.

"Well, never mind, we'll just cut them in half," Cook declared.

Sophie laughed. "That's what I figured."

"What are you doing still standing here? Go get washed up. I'm going to need you to do the slicing. You're the only one who will make sure there's no fighting."

Sophie laughed again. "Yes, I'll be sure to make the cuts even." She hurried to the door, calling over her shoulder as she went. "I'll be as quick as a bunny."

The grumpy overseer of the kitchens barely cracked a smile at her as she rushed away. Sophie didn't care. The man was her family. She had known him since she had arrived at the age of ten. She actually loved his gruff grumpiness. It never wavered. It gave her a sense of security. She never had to wonder what mood he would be in. His growl was almost comforting. It was home.

With a grin, Sophie ran up the stairs to her room. Within moments she had washed her face and hands and was back in the kitchen with an apron on, a sharp knife in her hand, and a pile of sliced doughnuts growing beside her.

Chapter 2

Renton stared at the urchin holding the door. "What do you mean she's too busy to come to the door? Did you tell her my name?"

When the child nodded vigorously, Renton asked suspiciously, "Are you sure?"

"I'm surer than sure, sir. Mr. Renton Rexford the Third, you said, sir, and that's what I said. But she said she can't come to the door." The child shrugged. "Nothing I can do about that, mister."

There was nothing Renton could do either. It was most peculiar. This was the third day in a row that Sophie had brushed him off. The first day, he had at least seen her as she was rushing off to do some sort of errand, but for the last two days, when he had knocked at the door, she had refused to see him. He knew she was always kept busy with her work here at the orphanage, but it wasn't like her to refuse to so much as greet him.

She's never been this busy before, he grumbled to himself, while he wondered if she had lost interest in him and was being too kind to tell him so. *Not that it's really a kindness to keep me dangling on a string*, he grumbled some more. *No*, he thought, *she is far too forthright for that.* She would have the honesty to tell him if she didn't want him calling on her anymore, he was sure of it.

Standing on the sidewalk, staring up at the unimpressive, large building, Renton wrinkled his nose. Perhaps he ought to volunteer there in order to lift some of the burden from her slim shoulders. Surely if they had more help, Sophie wouldn't be too busy for him. With a nod, he set off for his parents' house. His mother would know who he needed to talk to. She was always involved in some form of fundraising for the various charities that were her pet projects. He knew the Foundling Hospital was one of them. That was how he had met Sophie in the first place.

Thus decided, his steps were lighter, and he whistled a merry tune as he turned toward his mother's house with long, purposeful strides. Glancing at his timepiece, he wagered he would be able to catch her having her tea before she left for her calls.

As he walked toward his mother's house, Renton thought about the last time he had spent time with Sophie. They had been "conveniently" running into each other at least once or twice a week ever since the fundraiser four months ago. Each time he got to spend time with her, he would make sure to ascertain what her schedule was for the upcoming days and make sure he was on the same street or attending the same event. She had been participating in some of the fundraising efforts for the orphanage so that had made it even easier to be with her. It had been just such an event, organized by his mother, at which he had seen her the week before.

She had looked stunning, as usual, as she scurried around doing his mother's bidding, finishing up the myriad last minute details that his mother always left undone. Renton had been amazed at Sophie's patience with his mother's constant dictates. When he had commented about it to Sophie, all she had done was smile serenely. "I'm willing to do just about anything for the orphanage, Renton, surely you realize that. Fetching a few things for your mother is really nothing for me to object to. She does so much good for the children. I can only be grateful to her."

Renton couldn't really argue with her reasoning but finally, halfway through the evening, he had insisted she had done enough.

"My mother has actual paid staff, Sophie. They can look after things for the rest of the evening. Come dance with me. You are looking far too pretty to be wasting your time back here in the kitchens."

The way she had blushed and stammered and then spent the rest of the evening by his side had made Renton think she was just as happy in his company as he was in hers, but the way she was now avoiding him was making him wonder if he had somehow offended her. His chest felt tight at the thought. Meeting her this winter had been the best thing that ever happened to him. He had to get to the bottom of her changed behavior.

He tried to think over every detail of that last evening. They had discussed some of Wordsworth's poems as well as Alexandre Dumas' latest book. Renton always enjoyed listening to her enthusiastic descriptions of her favorite bits when they'd both read something. He would rather hear her describe the book than read it himself. Her interesting way of elaborating on it was far better than what his own imagination could conjure. They'd also had a rather heated discussion about the Baltimore Female College that had just opened a few years ago in order to educate teachers. It was not that he didn't think she was capable of doing the studies, far from it, he just didn't want her going away for such a long time. He thought he had made that clear. But maybe after she thought about it afterward she had decided he was too wrongheaded for her to deal with.

Renton shook his head. Sophie would have the courage to tell him to his face if she thought he was wrong; he was sure of it. *But what could it be?* She had seemed so happy that night. There was no indication of anything that would lead her to severing contact with him. Maybe he was reading too much into her refusal to see him that morning. Maybe she really was just too busy to come to the door.

The walk from the orphanage to his mother's house was further than he had anticipated, but the time passed quickly as he thought more about that night. The only time he had seen Sophie's smile dim was as she had taken leave of his mother. Renton had been caught up in a conversation with a business associate so he had not accompanied Sophie as she went to speak with her hostess. He found it hard to believe his mother would have reprimanded Sophie for not continuing to run about for her all evening. Sophie had already done so much before Renton had whisked her away to the dance floor. But Renton knew his mother didn't always consider people to be her equal. She could be a little snobby at times, thinking those of less means were also of less worth. But no, his mother surely wouldn't have said anything untoward to Sophie.

Sophie was such a darling, no one could have anything less than kind to say to her.

Upon arrival at his parents' home, Renton had been right in his assessment of his mother's whereabouts. He asked for her when the door was opened by one of her maids.

"She's just having her tea, sir. I'm sure she'll be glad to see you. Would you like me to take your coat?"

"Thank you," he answered, distracted by the fact that he couldn't remember her name.

She smiled politely and led him to his mother's parlour. "Your son is here to see you, ma'am."

"Renton, darling, what a wonderful surprise. Bring a fresh pot and another cup, Maisie," she called out as the maid was leaving. Maisie didn't bother answering, she just dipped a small curtsy and hurried away to do Mrs. Rexford's bidding.

"Good morning, Mother. How are you today? I'm glad I found you at home."

"I'm even better than I was now that you have arrived," his mother answered coyly and he strove not to roll his eyes.

There was an awkward silence wherein his mother must have realized she had gone a little far. She quickly asked, "To what do I owe the pleasure of having you arrive unannounced and unsummoned?"

Now Renton really did roll is eyes. But his mother was right, he pretty much never visited anymore without a summons. After his disrespectful eye roll, his face creased into a grin. It wasn't possible to remain serious with his mother.

"I need some information, and I am certain you are the best one to ask."

"Really?" Her eyes sparkled at his words. "How can I help you?"

"I want to volunteer at the Foundling Hospital. With whom should I speak in order to make the arrangements?"

He would have laughed at the shocked look on her face if he wasn't so serious about needing access to the Hospital, and therefore access to Sophie.

"I don't understand your question, my son," she began carefully. "Do you wish to make a donation?"

"No, I am certain our family donates quite enough. I would like to actually do some work there. Surely they accept volunteer help." He was becoming frustrated with her lack of understanding.

"But why? We help with donations. We don't actually go there."

Renton had always suspected this was her attitude but was surprised to hear her actually express it. "Now I have to confess that I don't understand. Why wouldn't you want to go there? Are you not always talking about how much you help the less fortunate in the city?"

"Well of course we help. We just don't do it in person. That is for others to do, Renton. Surely you are too busy and too important to go down there. It is so very dirty and vulgar."

"Mother, I am shocked by your reaction. Haven't you ever wanted to see for yourself what you're involved in with your charities?"

His mother let out a tinkling laugh that Renton had the sinking suspicion was less than sincere. "Not at all, my son. Our family has been very fortunate, so we share that with others. That doesn't mean we need to get personal about it."

Renton blinked. While he had occasionally suspected his mother was shallow in her interests, he had never realized she was so very insincere in her charitable works. "Well, I want to get personal about it," Renton insisted.

"This is about that girl, isn't it?" his mother demanded shrewdly. "She told you what I said, didn't she?"

Feeling all the hairs on the back of his neck stand on end, Renton demanded, "What girl? Sophie? What did you say to her?"

He saw a flash of discomfort cross her face. "I don't know what you're talking about," she tried to prevaricate.

Renton sighed. "You said, and I quote, 'she told you what I said, didn't she'. Was the *she* you are referring to Sophie? What did you say to her?"

"I don't care for your tone, Renton Rexford. I am your mother."

"Yes, you are my mother, but I am a grown man. You cannot control my life any longer, Mother. Now, respectfully, tell me what you said to her."

His mother narrowed her eyes at him while looking down her nose as haughtily as she could manage. "I think it is time for you to leave, Son. I have things to attend to."

Renton sighed again. Clearly, he wasn't going to get anywhere with her in this mood. But he now really knew enough. It was obvious she had said something off putting to Sophie, which was why she would no longer walk with him comfortably. He needed to get himself inside the Foundling Hospital. If he could make Sophie see him as a real companion rather than his mother's son, he had a much better chance of getting somewhere with her. Or at least he hoped so. His stomach clenched at the thought of losing her affections. He had to do something.

Chapter 3

Sophie felt her eyes widen. She didn't care if she looked like an owl blinking in shock. She could hardly believe the sight before her.

"What are you doing here?" she demanded as Mr. Rexford turned and grinned. Sophie had to bite her lip not to grin at him in return. He was draped in an apron, which looked incongruous over his neatly pressed shirt and tie — along with his shiny black shoes peeking out from the bottom. But just seeing him in her own familiar place caused a flurry of emotions to ripple through her. A part of her was excited to have him there in her home and a frisson of attraction shivered up her spine. But another part of her needed to protect her home. The Foundling Hospital was the only place of security she had ever known, and she needed to make sure that didn't change. That overrode everything. It didn't matter that the man was deliciously handsome. She didn't want him there.

But how could she get him to leave? A delicate balance needed to be struck. It would not do to offend the deep-pocketed Rexfords. She would need to make him think it was his idea, she supposed. *But how to accomplish that?* she wondered.

She started with a tentative smile to the room at large, since no one had bothered to reply to her demand as to what Mr. Rexford was doing in the orphanage's kitchen. Since he was covered in an apron, it was obvious he wasn't merely there to check on his family's donations. Or maybe he was. Maybe that wasn't so very obvious. Maybe he was just the hands on sort who wanted to see for himself how his contributions were being used. Not that she had ever heard of anyone doing that, but she supposed it was as reasonable an explanation as any as to why the handsome young man had suddenly turned up in the orphanage kitchen.

In fact, perhaps she ought to apologize for her outburst. Otherwise he might be tempted to pull the family's considerable funds. Sophie stifled a sigh. She didn't actually know what would be the best thing to do at this moment.

Sophie finally determined that the best thing, for the moment at least, would be to ignore all her uncertainties since it didn't seem as though anyone was about to offer her any answers. With another vague smile to the room at large, when she realized everyone was still gazing at her, she stepped briskly into the room. Grabbing her own large apron, Sophie covered herself from neck to ankle and made her way toward the table. Without looking at Mr. Rexford again, she set to work chopping. After a moment's hesitation, everyone else resumed their work as well, following her lead.

The morning passed with remarkably little eventuality. Sophie kept glancing toward Renton and was surprised to see how well he was doing with each task Cook assigned him. Her ears perked up as he began whistling a jaunty tune as he chopped. It was no time at all before everyone had finished their assigned tasks.

"That was much harder than I had expected."

Sophie nearly jumped out of her skin, she was so startled by the deep, low voice coming over her shoulder. She had been so aware of him all morning, she was shocked that she hadn't notice him approach her as she checked on the last-minute touches as they finished making the children's lunch.

"Sorry to have startled you."

He didn't look sorry as he grinned down at her. Sophie bit her lip in order to quell her emotions. She wasn't sure if it was irritation or attraction that fluttered uppermost in her chest, but it wouldn't do to be displaying either.

After drawing a deep breath to quell her feelings, she offered him a small smile. "So, how did you come to be working in our kitchen this morning?"

"Cassandra Morley's mother is a friend of my mother. I remembered my mother mentioning to me that Cass was volunteering here, so I called on her and she made the arrangements."

Sophie had to exert effort to keep her smile in place as she felt herself turning green with envy over the comfortable way he discussed the other young woman. Cassie was lovely and Sophie would actually say they were friends, but in that moment it was a struggle to remember that fact.

"How nice," she managed to say. Sophie was hoping to be able to scurry away, now that their task had been concluded, but she needed to avoid being overtly rude to the generous man.

Before she was able to make her escape, he prompted her with another question. "Do you always prepare so very much? Or was that for my benefit, since you had an extra pair of hands?"

Sophie had to laugh. "Actually, you weren't extra. Normally two other women are helping in the kitchen, but they were busy today, making preparations for the train ride next week."

At his quizzical look, Sophie explained. "Don't you know about Mr. Brace's new initiative to send some of the orphans on the train out to farming families in the west?"

When Renton shook his head, Sophie elaborated. "I will try not to bore you with too many details, but it is a wonderfully exciting opportunity for the children he has selected. He has already sent out two groups of children, and they were all successfully placed with families to look after them. This time we're going as far as the train tracks go. All the way to Missouri!"

"What is the purpose of this?" Renton seemed puzzled, but genuinely interested.

"Mr. Brace believes that farm families all have room for at least one more place at the table and could all use a hand with working their land. Since here in New York so many children have lost their parents to different things, he's sending them out of the city to new lives, lives where they have a chance for a new family."

"You seem pretty excited about it. Do you wish you had been sent on the train when you lost your parents?"

Sophie forced a laugh despite her discomfort. "The train didn't go anywhere when I lost my parents. But every orphan dreams of having a family."

Renton's face filled with sympathy, and Sophie had to fight so that her eyes didn't fill with tears. But then he interrupted his own thoughts with a question. "Wait, you said *we* are going as far as Missouri. What did you mean? Are you moving away?"

Sophie's laugh was much more genuine this time. "Not at all. I still love New York despite everything. No, I'm not moving, but the children cannot just be loaded on the train and left to themselves. It will take almost two weeks to get all the way to the end of the line. A few of us who work or volunteer here will be accompanying the children to their new lives."

"So how long will you be gone?" To Sophie's ears he actually sounded angry at the thought of her being away. Her heart wanted to soar with that knowledge, but she frowned to quell the impulse.

"About a month. Our return tickets haven't been arranged. It will depend on how long we remain with the children when we reach our destination. And of course, with any type of travel, despite all the wonderful innovations, you can never be completely sure if things won't go wrong." She paused when she noticed his scowl.

"Are you all right, Mr. Rexford?"

His face cleared at her question. "Yes, of course, I'm fine. I just worry a little bit about you going off on this train ride."

Sophie could feel her eyebrows reaching toward her hairline.

He quickly added, "I'm not questioning your competence, Miss Brooks, I assure you. It is just, as you said, things can go wrong and you never know who else might be traveling in the same direction."

Sophie laughed. "Well, I never said that last bit. But I am fully confident that Katie, Melanie, Mrs. Parker, and I shall be just fine."

"Only women?"

Sophie laughed again, although this time it was a bit more forced. "Very competent women."

He had the grace to flush. "Of course. I'm sure you are all highly competent. But are you not nervous about it? What if something goes wrong?"

"Things go wrong every day of the week, Mr. Rexford. I am well aware of that. And well experienced in the matter of dealing with all those misfortunes that come our way. Mrs. Parker and I have already had this experience a couple times already. This will be Katie and Melanie's first time. And in fact, they won't be returning to New York. That is why they aren't here today. They have to tie up any loose ends of their lives here before heading west."

He was quiet for a moment while he gazed at her as though he were assessing her. "Are you absolutely certain you are coming back?"

"Absolutely," Sophie repeated. Part of her wanted to demand what business it was of his, but she couldn't bear to hear the answer, whatever it might be. *He is not for you,* she reminded herself with as much fervor as she could muster, *remember what is at stake.* That finally brought her to her senses. She could feel the color draining from her face. With a tight smile, she tried to make her escape.

"Your help was certainly appreciated this morning, sir. I must be going to complete the rest of my chores."

He tried to stop her. "Can I help you?"

Sophie wanted to be elsewhere. "It would probably be best if you speak to Mrs. Parker," she said, desperate to be away, and finally turned on her heel and fled, uncaring if he thought her rude.

CB80CB80

Renton watched as Sophie rushed away. He was more confused than ever. He knew girls could be contrary creatures, but she was worse than any he had ever met. He had thought they were attracted to one another. At the very least, he had thought they were friends. Even today, there were moments when he had been certain she was enjoying his company, and then she turned around and ran off on him. He frowned as he looked in the direction in which she had departed. Should he chase after her? It would hardly be appropriate since he rather suspected the bedrooms were located up the stairs she had climbed. It would also hardly be seemly. He could just hear his mother now. 'Rexfords do not need to pursue relationships, Renton, dear, surely you know that.'

But he *wanted* to pursue a relationship with Sophie. Despite their being from different stations in life, he found her company far more engaging than that of any other female of his acquaintance. She was well read and articulate despite not having attended finishing school or moving about within his usual social circle. Besides, he thought, this is America. His mother was always going on about how their name means Son of a King, but he rather doubted they were of legitimate birth. And very few of their friends were of noble birth. Of course, many were the sons of younger sons of the nobility back in England, but what did that matter? To his mind, being clever enough to make your own way was what mattered. Just like his father had managed to do, making his fortune from small beginnings. Even he, himself, didn't have anything to boast about. Being his father's son meant that, while he prided himself on working hard, he had a position ready made for him by his father. Sophie, on the other hand, had so many things working against her in her young life, but look at her. She managed to keep a joyful disposition and worked hard for the benefit of others. He was proud to call her his friend. Or so he had thought. He sighed and went in search of Mrs. Parker as Sophie had admonished him.

"Oh, Mr. Rexford, how has your morning been so far? I must say, I could hardly believe it when Cassie told me you wanted to help out here in a literal way. We are always open to extra hands, but today it was particularly helpful."

Renton cleared his throat, a little uncomfortable with the woman's effusive praise. "Yes, Miss Brooks mentioned that a couple women who would normally be here were tied up today."

"Yes, such dear girls. Katie and Melanie had some things to take care of today." Mrs. Parker looked disinclined to elaborate.

"I suppose you will be particularly short-staffed when you are away escorting the children on the train." Renton was well aware that he was prying, but it didn't strike him as being rude. As a donor to the orphanage, he *was* interested in its smooth operation. And he *did* actually care about the welfare of the orphans. Really, what was going to happen when four of the usual caretakers were absent?

Now Mrs. Parker had begun to look harried. "Yes, of course, but there will be far fewer children to care for as well. Mr. Brace has it well in hand." There was a pause while she appeared to struggle with how to handle him.

Renton wanted to laugh but controlled the impulse. It was obvious the poor woman wasn't used to dealing with donors on a personal level. It struck Renton as odd that his mother and her cronies had never actually stepped in to help in a literal way.

Mrs. Parker surprised him with her next inquiry. "Are you offering to make yourself available, Mr. Rexford? It would be a beneficial experience for the children, especially the boys. We appreciate any offer of assistance from whatever quarter it comes from, but it is pretty much only females who volunteer here. And even our employed staff is almost only female. In fact, I was going to suggest, if you intend to remain any longer, that you might wish to look in on some of the boys. Have you any experience with children, sir? If you knew of some games you could play with them, or if you thought you could help them with their lessons, it would be so very beneficial for them."

Renton hesitated. He had made arrangements to volunteer that day in order to gain access to Sophie, but that hadn't yet worked out the way he had hoped. And now, seeing how much help was truly needed, he wanted to do what he could, but he suddenly felt inadequate.

"I have several young cousins I've spent time with, but I'm not absolutely certain how I could be of assistance." He could hear the uncertainty in his voice and just barely managed not to cringe. He was not used to feeling incompetent. He was quickly questioning the wisdom of his visit.

"Anything you could manage would be just fine," Mrs. Parker soothed.

Again Renton had to suppress the urge to laugh. It was obvious the older woman was used to managing people. She was already coming around her desk and taking his arm, obviously enthused with the idea of his providing company to the children.

"There is still some time before lunch. Has anyone shown you around?" Without waiting for his response, she steered him out of the room and carried on talking. "Oh, the boys will be so happy to see you. Surely you must know some games they'll enjoy. It hasn't been so very long since you were a boy yourself, isn't that right, Mr. Rexford?"

Renton felt as though he were choking on his desire to laugh, but he was also torn between that and a gut-wrenching fear of facing the children all of a sudden. Before he could formulate a coherent objection, they had stepped into a large classroom. It wasn't like any classroom Renton had been in though. All the children were currently standing beside their desks, marching in place. The intruders hadn't made much, if any noise, especially not to be heard over the sound of many footsteps, but still, all heads turned in their direction, leaving Renton feeling awkward and out of place.

"Good morning, children, we have the pleasure of Mr. Rexford's company today. Who wants to tell him why you are all standing right now?"

Several hands began waving eagerly in the air.

"Tony, what can you tell us?"

"Teacher says we can learn better if we ain't, I mean, aren't having so many fidgets."

"Very good, Tony. Do you think it works?"

The child shrugged but grinned as he kept right on marching.

"Who would like to tell Mr. Rexford what you were learning this morning?"

Many more hands were now waving, much to Renton's surprise. When he had been in school, it had always seemed like no one wanted to participate. Renton was impressed. Obviously the strange methods were working.

"Ross?" Renton was now also impressed with Mrs. Parker's knowledge of the children and their names. He was certain there were at least 200 children in residence at the orphanage. The fact that Mrs. Parker knew the names of all the children, who looked like just a sea of faces to Renton's mind, told him that she either had a remarkable mind or truly cared about the children. From the scattered appearance of her office, he would be willing to bet money on it being the latter. That thought made him grin until the child stepped forward and started to explain their lessons.

"We're learning about villeinage and feudalism in the fourteenth and fifteen centuries," came the explanation from a small lad in the front of the room. To Renton's untrained eye he looked like he couldn't be much more than seven or eight years old.

"Good heavens, why?" he blurted without thinking. He didn't expect an answer but to his surprise, the small boy provided one.

"Teacher says to understand the past leads to a better future."

Renton cleared his throat. "Sounds to me like your teacher is a wise man."

The children were obviously growing restless with their curiosity but his statement resulted in grins and quiet cheers. Mrs. Parker's gaze was shrewd.

"Perhaps Mr. Rexford could stay with the class until you break for lunch," she stated to the teacher rather than asking either of them before she swept from the room.

Renton was at a momentary loss. He felt as though she had just thrown him to the wolves. Of course, they were only children, but he hadn't expected to be left with the full focus of what felt like hundreds of children. In actuality, it was probably only thirty, but it certainly felt overwhelming as he returned their steady gazes.

Thankfully, the teacher came to his rescue.

"Very good, boys. Now, take your seats and we'll try for a little more instruction before the bell rings for lunch."

Renton watched, fascinated, as the teacher managed to regain the full attention of the classroom and he really did lead them in learning something more. Before he knew it, there was a loud ringing. It was time for lunch. He could hardly believe how quickly the morning had flown. Despite feeling exhausted, he was sure it had been the most enjoyable morning he had experienced in ages. And it wasn't just the opportunity to see Sophie that had made him so happy, he realized as he spotted her across the large room when he accompanied the boys down to lunch. Their eyes met and he was surprised to feel a flutter of excitement. Of course, he knew he was attracted to her, but he hadn't felt this type of awareness since he was a lad first discovering that girls were pretty. It made him nervous. He was torn between running toward her and running away like a coward. He was saved from ignominy by the urchin at his side.

"Hey, mister. Wanna eat lunch with me?"

The small boy couldn't have been more than five or six. Although since he looked like he hadn't been properly fed for most of his life, it was entirely possible he was older than he looked. But the resigned look on his face as though he expected life to throw another disappointment at him, made him look ancient. And made Renton unable to refuse.

"I would enjoy that very much, thank you for asking," he answered politely, making the boys around him laugh and giggle like the children they were. Renton's heart went out to them. It was coming home to him just how very unfair life truly was.

He looked across the room briefly and saw Sophie's intense interest. He wasn't sure what his smile might have told her. He wasn't completely sure what he was feeling himself. But her return smile was warm and encouraging.

Lunch passed in a blur. He could hardly keep up with all the chatter as each little boy tried to outdo the other as they entertained him with their stories. Renton couldn't be sure how much was truth and how much exaggeration, but if even a fraction were true, the youngsters had all led colorful, traumatic lives.

That afternoon, he joined another one of the teachers who was focusing on physical education for the children.

"We try to keep the children occupied as much as possible so they aren't tempted to return to their former lives."

"What do you mean, their former lives? Aren't their parents dead? There's no going back to their former lives." Renton was confused.

"Most of the children, the boys especially, have spent time on the streets before coming to us at the orphanage. Most of them have been forced here after running into trouble with authorities. Very few of them were happy about winding up in an orphanage. They had made communities or families for themselves out on the streets. Most are resistant to following rules after the freedom they have experienced. Or they have dealt with terrible abuse in their past and trust no one. Either way, they resist being here for the most part. Running around and being occupied helps them to focus on the merits of being here. And keeps them from causing us too much trouble."

Renton hadn't realized the children wouldn't want to be there. Of course, it would make sense that they would rather have their families back. But if their families were dead, there wasn't much that could be done about that. Being at the orphanage struck him as the lesser of evils. But the teacher's explanation made sense, and Renton looked at the children and the service being provided by the orphanage in a new light. He was all the more determined to do whatever he could to help out. He nearly ran himself ragged playing with each classroom of children as they changed throughout the afternoon.

Renton was a little embarrassed when Sophie came across him as he was gasping for air, hanging over the balustrade late that afternoon. She laughed and asked, "Have the children worn you out, Mr. Rexford?"

"Yes!" he answered simply but he returned her grin. "I fear I did not dress properly for the exertions of the day."

Sophie glanced down and winced. "I don't think your feet will appreciate what you've been doing."

"No, they don't, but it has been worth every blister I'm sure to have."

"Really, Mr. Rexford? I didn't really picture you as being the hands on type."

Renton was hurt by her words but thought that might explain her strange behavior. His feelings must have displayed themselves on his face because she suddenly started blushing.

"Is that why you have been avoiding me? You don't think I could share your interest in the orphans?" he asked.

He watched, fascinated as the color in her cheeks deepened further. "I haven't been avoiding you," she protested.

"Liar," he said to her, keeping his voice firm even though part of him wanted to tease her for her discomfort. She was so appealing. He needed to know why she was trying to distance herself from him.

Sophie's eyes darted everywhere but toward his own gaze as she clearly struggled to formulate a response. Renton felt bad for making her uncomfortable, but he held silent in the hopes that she would explain herself. When tears filled her eyes, though, it was the last reaction he had expected.

"Sophie, what is it? Surely you can tell me."

"I can't," she said, her voice wretched. Without saying anything else, she gathered her skirts and ran away.

Despite his sore feet, Renton did his best to chase after her.

Chapter 4

Sophie tried to get away from Renton, but she was choking on the tears she was trying to hold back. She almost tripped over her own feet as she hurried away. The pain in his feet didn't seem to be encumbering him over much as he quickly caught up to her. They were just outside an empty classroom when he grabbed her arm and pulled her inside.

"Sophie," he said in a soft tone. His deep voice contained only compassion and questions, making Sophie feel all the more desperate. She had so many feelings for him, but she just couldn't tell him the truth. She tried to get herself back under control. There was too much at stake for her to give in to her own weak emotions.

"Sophie, my dear, you must tell me."

She tried to brazen it out. Sophie pulled herself together and raised her chin. There was barely a wobble in her voice as she began to speak. "You really don't have any claims over me,

Mr. Rexford. You have no right to tell me what I must or must not do. And I do not appreciate you calling me a liar."

His searching gaze studied her face, and Sophie fought to remain impassive. She wasn't sure if she had been successful when his puzzled frown remained compassionate instead of withdrawing as she had hoped.

"I thought we were friends," he said, remaining calm and kind.

"What made you think that, Mr. Rexford?" Sophie was hoping for a cold tone but the remaining teariness in her voice put a lie to her efforts.

He was still holding her arm, which was a relief and a torment all at once. She was so distraught she might have sunk to the floor without his support, but his warm grasp on her arm was interfering with her efforts to be stolid and firm. He smiled, apparently not put out in the least by her efforts to distance herself from him.

"What made me think we were friends?" He repeated her question after a few beats. "Perhaps it was the way my heart lifts every time you are near, or the way your face lights up when our eyes meet across a crowded room. Or maybe it's the long conversations we have whenever our paths cross, as though we're two halves of a whole. Even when we disagree our conversations are enjoyable."

As he was talking, Sophie's breath caught in the back of her throat and her heart sped up. She desperately wanted to throw herself into his arms and beg him to stay her friend. But she couldn't. She had to think of the children.

Her heart shrank within her chest and her chin wobbled as her eyes filled with tears, but she lifted her chin and looked him right in the face as she told him, "Well, Mr. Rexford, you thought wrong. We are not friends. We cannot be friends. You are a wealthy business man. I am an orphan working at the Foundling Hospital. No friendship is possible between us. And I would ask that you unhand me so that I can carry on with my day."

Renton blinked and his face fell. For a moment, Sophie's heart sank and she wanted to throw up, as she thought she had been successful in her attempts to end their fledgling relationship. His hand loosened on her arm and she was about to pull away from him. But then he tightened it and brought his other hand up to grasp her left arm. He wasn't hurting her, but it was evident he would not be letting her go.

"No, Sophie. I don't believe you. I *know* you. And this is so unlike you that I know there must be something else going on. What did my mother say to you?"

Sophie gasped as she felt all the color drain away from her face and she was suddenly light headed. "How do you know about that? Renton, please, you cannot say anything to her."

"So there *is* something. Out with it, Sophie. You know we're friends. And you know I won't let this go. Tell me what is going on."

She had tried so hard to be strong and it was all falling down around her feet. The tears she had been trying to hold back slipped silently down her cheeks. If she wasn't so caught up in her own misery, she would have enjoyed the wretched look on his face as he despaired over her distress.

"It's bigger than us, Renton. It's the children. All of the children. I cannot. You have to try to understand. You've been here all day. You've seen the children. I cannot allow this to be taken away." Her words bolstered her own determination. Her spine got its steel back, and her tears dried. Sophie stepped away from his suddenly loosened grasp. It would have been funny to see his mouth gaping in shock if it wasn't such a deadly serious situation.

Her heart was breaking but her determination was stronger than ever. She was about to sweep from the room, running away to find somewhere private to scream and sob. But before she could leave, his hand clamped on her arm once more and he spun her to face him.

"Are you saying my mother has threatened the orphanage? How?"

"No, I'm not telling you anything. Please, Renton, let this go. Let *me* go. There's nothing for us to pursue here." She was prepared to beg if she had to. She just wanted to get away and nurse her emotional injuries.

"There's plenty for us to pursue. I wasn't mistaken. We *are* friends. Maybe we could even be more than friends. I am not prepared to just let this go."

Sophie's resolve hardened further and her chin raised to a stubborn level. "Any friend of mine would not jeopardize something that I hold so dear."

Renton's stance softened. "Sophie, my dear, you know I won't allow my mother to do anything to this place."

"How do you think you could possibly stop her? No one can force her where to put her charitable donations. The Foundling Hospital and the Children's Aid Society are completely dependent on the munificence of others." Sophie could feel her chin trembling with the force of her tumultuous emotions, but she held it at a firm angle. "This has been my home since I was ten years old. I depend on it. But I am a grown woman at this point. I could manage. But the little ones cannot. I cannot take the chance on my actions harming their future."

Renton's stare was hard, making her squirm. "Tell me what she said to you. You owe me that at least."

Sophie couldn't look him in the eye as she finally told him the truth. She knew it would be awkward for him to hear that his mother was interfering in his life in such a way. "She said if I do not cut my ties with you, she will cut her funding efforts. She said there are many charities that would be happy to cooperate with her wishes. She also told me I wasn't to tell you so you really cannot say anything to her. Please, Renton, you must swear it to me."

He continued to stare hard at her. Sophie could almost see the wheels of thought turning in his head as she finally met his gaze. Slowly a gentle, beautiful smile bloomed on his face.

"If I can find a reliable solution to the funding problem, will you stop resisting my efforts to spend time with you?"

It seemed to Sophie as though her heart stopped for a moment before it began hammering madly within her chest. She wanted to throw herself into his arms, but she had to try to see sense.

"You cannot give your own money, Renton. Your mother would stop you. Besides, she gets so many other people to donate. I've seen the ledgers. It's too much."

"First of all, Sophie, darling, my mother doesn't have any say over how I spend my money. Even without the family funds, I do quite well for myself, have no fear. But I have another idea that just might work swimmingly. So I will repeat my question. Will you, Sophie Brooks, allow me to court you with serious intention if I can solve the problem of funding for the Foundling Hospital?"

Sophie finally allowed hope to flood into her heart. She could feel her cheeks stretching from the smile that bloomed on her face. She couldn't speak around the emotion clogging her throat, so she nodded tentatively. Renton whooped, picked her up, and spun her around in a circle. He put her back on her feet and then quickly planted a quick kiss softly on her lips.

She could only stare as he grinned at her. "I will return as soon as I have it all sorted," he promised her before rushing from the room.

With trembling fingers, Sophie covered her mouth and looked at the empty doorway through which he had disappeared. *Had it all been a dream?* With a shake of her head, she tried to pull her hopes back down to earth, but she couldn't prevent her smile from remaining fixed in place as she slowly made her way down to supper.

Chapter 5

Sophie remained on tenterhooks for three days. The hours dragged by as she went about her duties. For two days she could barely eat, but by the third day she took herself to task. *You are being absolutely ridiculous,* she told her reflection as she pulled her hair back into a severe style, jabbing pins in haphazardly, trying to regain a sense of control over something in her life, even if it was merely her unruly curls. *I told you not to get your hopes up. Look what it leads to. You are moping around here as though you have lost out on something. Nothing has been lost that you didn't already have. If you do not pull yourself together, you are going to give the children the vapors. Especially the children bound for the train.*

Thus admonished, she did indeed manage to get her emotions under a semblance of control. She managed to choke down at least some of the hearty breakfast placed before her, and she was able to smile sincerely at the little girl sitting next to her at the table.

"Are you excited about leaving on the train in a few days, Annie?"

The child's eyes were huge in her face as she turned her attention from her plate. "I think so, Miss Sophie."

Sophie actually laughed, although it was soft and brief. "Why aren't you sure?"

Annie scrunched her nose as she thought. "Well, I'm afeared, for one thing. I've never been on a train before. And none of my friends are going."

Sophie's heart ached for the child. Mr. Brace was sending very few girls on this trip. "You will make lots of friends in your new home, I'm sure."

The little girl nodded vigorously. "I sure hope so."

"So what are the positive things that make you think you might be excited about it?"

"Mrs. Parker said maybe my new family will let me have a kitten." The blissful smile that accompanied this statement made Sophie react with another laugh, this one much more sincere.

"That *is* powerful incentive for leaving, I would imagine."

"And it *will* be nice to have a mommy and daddy." The child's voice was wistful but not weak. Sophie was grateful the poor little girl's hope had not been completely squashed despite the tragedies she'd endured.

Sophie nodded and clasped the child's hand. There wasn't anything she could say to that. It was every orphan's heartfelt wish to belong to a family. She, herself, was too old to be wishing for parents but as she looked around the large room, she felt this was the closest she was going to get to having a family of her own. She had two hundred little brothers and sisters. And all the staff members were like aunts and uncles for her. But she did not begrudge the children leaving on the train their opportunity to get a family of their own. Nor the opportunity to have a kitten, she thought with a wistful smile. It would have been her own dearest wish when she was younger.

"There is nothing to fear about going on the train, though. I have been a couple of times already. It is actually rather spectacular. Before my first trip, I had never been outside of the city. You will be amazed at how vast everything feels as we ride by. We will drive through fields that feel like they go on and on for miles. And forests and streams and farms. It is really beautiful. And at night. Oh, Annie, wait until nighttime! You won't believe your eyes when you see the stars."

"Really, Miss Sophie? What else will we see?"

"Cows and sheep and horses and chickens."

Annie wrinkled her nose again. "Won't they be stinky?"

Sophie giggled and so did the little girl. "Well, you won't be able to smell the animals from the train, but I do have to tell you that the train itself is a little stinky. But when we get off the train when it stops from time to time, you won't believe how sweet the air smells. It's the one thing that makes me wish I was staying behind when the train heads back to the city."

Annie looked at her seriously for a moment, making Sophie's heart clench for the world of experience she could see in the youngster's gaze despite her few years of life. She was relieved when the little girl broke into a grin. "That sure sounds nice."

"Wait until you see it for yourself. I promise, you will love it."

With a grin and a wave, the child hurried off to wash her face and get ready for her classes. Watching her go, Sophie realized her own spirits had been lifted by their conversation. She was reminded of the important work she was involved in here with the orphans. If Renton never returned, it meant the funding from Mrs. Rexford was secured. She needed to keep her focus on the children and their needs. Her own were secondary at most. Thus resolved and restored to a measure of her usual cheer, she got to her feet and set about clearing up from the children. With the help of the older children whose assignment it was to help in the cafeteria that day, it wasn't long before they had the entire room squared away.

Sophie was just on her way to her next task when Cassandra Morley, one of the wealthy young woman who volunteered at the orphanage, approached her with a wide grin.

"Sophie! I've been looking for you. There's someone down in Mrs. Parker's office looking for you."

"Good morning, Cassie! Who is it?"

Cassie just shook her head and grinned. "You'll have to go and see for yourself."

Frowning, Sophie went to the kitchen to remove her apron before hurrying to Mrs. Parker's office. When she got there, Mrs. Parker too had a wide grin on her face.

"Sophie, my dear, Mr. Rexford here has a few things to discuss with you. You may feel free to use my office for as long as you need. I shall be in the east classroom if you need me."

Sophie hadn't noticed Renton was there when she first stepped into the room, but as soon as she caught sight of him, she barely noticed as Mrs. Parker left the room. The wide smile on his face and warm twinkle in his eyes made her heart skip a beat and the butterflies take flight in her stomach. But she tried to maintain a dignified façade.

"Mr. Rexford, you wished to see me?"

"Yes, Miss Brooks, I did." He kept his tone serious, to match hers, but she could see his lips twitching with amusement.

"Are you laughing at me again, Mr. Rexford?"

"Maybe just a little," he replied as he stepped forward and grasped her hand. "I've come to make sure you uphold your end of our bargain."

Sophie's stomach dipped and danced as her hopes took flight once more. She'd had her hopes dashed so many times in her young life, but her stupid heart refused to listen as Sophie tried to tell it to stay calm. She could feel tears gathering behind her eyes, but she wasn't sure if they were of joy or despair. Her lips trembled slightly as she took in a breath. Her nerves clenched more deliciously as she noticed his focus narrow on her lips before he dragged his gaze back to her eyes. She managed to find a smile.

"What bargain are you speaking about, Mr. Rexford?" She needed him to spell it out for her. She couldn't afford any assumptions.

"You promised to allow me to court you if I could ensure that you and the children would be safe from my mother's interference."

She had to smile over the gentle way he paraphrased her fears and emphasized his request for a courtship. Her heart clenched with the depth of her feelings for the man. She couldn't do anything but nod.

"Is that a yes, that you are still amenable to my courtship?" Sophie couldn't believe that he would even need to ask.

"Of course, I am," she answered with a laugh.

With a chuckle, he stepped forward, grabbed her and twirled her around in a tight circle, mindful of her skirts in the small, crowded room. Sophie allowed her joy to bubble up into laughter, but she forced herself to remain cautious as he restored her to feet.

"So? What solution have you found to solve the issues at hand? Were you able to convince your mother?"

Renton shrugged. "I did speak with her briefly this morning before coming here, merely to tell her that if she wanted to maintain a place in my life and that of any future grandchildren, she would have to ensure that she was pleasant to whomever I chose to share my life."

Sophie blinked as her heart soared and sank all at once. It was lovely to hear a man declaring his feelings, or rather she supposed, implying them. But she couldn't find her own happiness at the sacrifice of the children. She didn't know what to say. Her wrought feelings must have been written on her face because Renton was quick to continue as he maintained his hold on her hands, squeezing them gently as though in admonition for her doubts.

"The wife of one of the business partners in our firm, I'm not sure if you've met her, Mrs. Fitzhugh, a delightful woman, you'll enjoy her when you've become friends. Anyhow, she is in a constant rivalry with my mother. I visited her two days ago, and she was fascinated to hear about the good works being done by Mr. Brace and the Society. She will arrange a time for you to give her a tour when we go there for tea next week. I visited her again yesterday to hear all the details of the gala she has already made plans for to raise the needed funds to maintain the orphanage for the foreseeable future. Of course, I happened to mention this to my mother when I visited with her for a coffee this morning, so now she is in a tizzy of epic strategizing how she can arrange an even more successful fundraiser than

Mrs. Fitzhugh. To benefit the Children's Aid Society, of course. So you see, my darling, the orphanage and Mr. Brace's Society will now have at least twice as much funding than it had, and it's all thanks to you."

Sophie broke into a fit of giggles. "Well, I rather think it is thanks to you. I will have to remember never to cross you. You are devious beyond belief but even more brilliant than I had realized."

Renton bowed comically to her before growing serious once more. "So, once again, I will remind you, you and the children are now safe. I was happy to be of assistance to the dear orphans, and I have no intention of coercing you into a courtship with me, despite my words of a bargain. But, please, my dear Miss Sophie, do say you will allow it."

With a grin, Sophie dipped into a curtsy. "I would be honored, kind sir."

Renton grinned. "There's just one other thing, and I truly hope you don't think I am trying to take over control of your life because I promise you that I'm not. I know you are a smart, independent woman. It is actually one of the things I love about you, so I wouldn't want to take that away."

Sophie's joy led her to laugh again at his rambling. "Just say it, Renton, I promise to withhold judgment until you've explained yourself."

Renton smiled but maintained a worried mien. "It's about your trip on the train. I was so hoping you would agree to let me court you, and even that we could keep it short and sweet and soon begin our life together, you see, so I spoke to Cass Morley."

Sophie was again torn between a soaring heart and a frown over his words. "What do you mean?"

"She agreed that if you want to remain here, she would be happy to take your place with the children on the train."

"Really?" Her frown fled and Renton pulled her close again.

"Really. If you still want to go, I will try to maintain my patience. I will wait for you as long as you need, but I would ever so much rather get on with our future."

Sophie's heart fluttered and delicious shivers made their way down her spine, but she tried to keep a serious expression. "Do you have our future planned already, Mr. Rexford? I thought you promised me a courtship."

"I do promise you a courtship, my darling. One that will curl your toes with delight, I vow to you. But do not doubt that I have already made up my mind about you. The only purpose of the courtship is for you to be sure about me." He grinned sheepishly at her. "I don't want to scare you off, but you *have* met my mother. You aren't getting the very best bargain with me."

Sophie's joyful heart turned over in her chest, and she placed her palm gently on his cheek. "I beg to differ, Renton. You're the best bargain I will ever make."

With a soft whoop of joy, Renton bent his head and sealed their deal with a fervent kiss.

The End

If you enjoyed this story, you will love the rest of the *Orphan Train* series

Book no. 2 is:

She ran away and found home

Stay in touch with Wendy May Andrews and forthcoming publishing news.

Sign up for her biweekly newsletter on wendymayandrews.com

A Note From the Author:

This is a work of fiction but it *could* have happened. Mr. Charles Brace really was one of the founders of the Children's Aid Society. I took a little bit of liberty with the timing. The Foundling Hospital and The Children's Aid Society would've been new in 1854, but in this story, Sophie has lived there for 10 years. But the train really did go to the middle of Missouri in 1854 and Mr. Brace really did send children out west to be adopted and have, what he hoped would be, better lives. I really loved his philosophy of farmers having room for one more at their table.

I hope you enjoyed Sophie's story. Cassandra Morley's story is next.

She ran away and found home

New York City debutante, Cassandra Morley has grown close to a trio of young brothers while volunteering at an orphanage. When the three boys are sent on the train to Missouri to be adopted, she accompanies them despite how displeased her high society family is likely to be.

Single rancher, Charles Ainsworth, is glad to be in a position to provide a new home for three brothers. He has no use for the citified young woman who keeps stopping by to check on them, despite how beautiful he finds her. He feels obligated to tolerate her visits to please his new sons.

Their differences cause them to fight their attraction to one another, but when one of the boys goes missing, they have to learn to trust each other in order to bring him home.

To buy please visit wendymayandrews.com

Can she risk love without sacrificing her independence?

When Katie's husband and baby died, she vowed to never face such heartache again. Accompanying a trainload of orphans to their new lives in Missouri affords Katie the opportunity to start a new life of her own. She jumps at the chance, determined to grab life with both hands.

Doctor Wyatt Jeffries doesn't appreciate Katie's independence and determination. Having had his heart broken when his first wife's illness turned her into a hard-hearted hellion, Wyatt is looking for a wife who will be happy staying home and raising babies. So he doesn't understand why he can't stop thinking about the town's new seamstress.

When the deadly threat of a mysterious illness looms, Katie and Wyatt are forced to work together to save their town. Is there any chance they can save their own hearts too?

To buy please visit wendymayandrews.com

Two challenged hearts. One true love?

The death of her mother left ten-year-old Melanie Jones with too many responsibilities. Raising her younger siblings under the weight of her father's unkind words filled her with insecurities. Despite those early years, she's determined to make a new life for herself. Moving far away from home, she boards a train to escort the latest load of orphans to Missouri.

Abandoned by his wife then widowed, Cole Miller is forced to raise his daughter on his own. Though his sister is supposed to help, she's more liability than asset. When a beautiful newcomer arrives in town, her doubts and insecurities leave Cole uninterested. He's had his fill of women like his wife and sister.

When Melanie steps in to help Cole with his daughter, he's able to see beyond her timidity and discover her beautiful and gracious soul. Will his discovery be enough for him to let go of his own uncertainties? Is Melanie ready for a family of her own?

To buy please visit wendymayandrews.com

About the Author

I've been writing pretty much since I learned to read when I was five years old. Of course, those early efforts were basically only something a mother could love ;-) I put writing aside after I left school and stuck with reading. I am an avid reader. I love words. I will read anything, even the cereal box, signs, posters, etc. But my true love is novels.

About ten years ago my husband dared me to write a book instead of always reading them. I didn't think I'd be able to do it, but to my surprise I love writing. Those early efforts eventually became my first published book – Tempting the Earl (published by Avalon books in 2010). There were some ups and downs in my publishing efforts. My first publisher was sold and I became an "orphan" author, back to the drawing board of trying to find a publishing house. It has been a thrilling adventure as I learned to navigate the world of publishing.

There are so many things that inspire me to write – an overheard conversation, dreams, a sappy commercial, a newspaper article. I write historical romance so I often think of various situations: "How would this work in 1805 or 1854?" and there's a story idea!

I believe firmly that everyone deserves a happily ever after. I want my readers to be able to escape from the everyday for a little while and feel upbeat and refreshed when they get to the end of my books. I hope you enjoyed Sophie's happy ending with me.

www.ingramcontent.com/pod-product-compliance
Lightning Source LLC
Chambersburg PA
CBHW021749190726
48290CB00008B/2549